Stories from Scotland

The stories in this book are some of the
old stories of Scotland, handed down by
storytellers for hundreds of years.

There are stories of great warriors and
strong magic, of a soldier who deserted
his regiment, a young girl who found a
fortune, and a young man who found a
bride. Yet each of these stories has a
meaning for today.

James Robertson Justice, who lives in
the Scottish Highlands, told them in
Jackanory.

STORIES FROM SCOTLAND

As told in Jackanory by

James Robertson Justice

Illustrated by Graham McCallum
British Broadcasting Corporation

Published by the British Broadcasting Corporation
35 Marylebone High Street, London W.1

SBN: 563 07453 1

© British Broadcasting Corporation 1968

First published 1968   Reprinted 1969, 1972

Printed in England by Hazell Watson & Viney Ltd.,
Aylesbury, Bucks

Contents

The Fairy Flag
of Dunvegan

On the island of Skye, off the west coast of
Scotland, stands the castle of Dunvegan. The
castle has been the home of the chiefs of the
Macleod family for hundreds of years.

Long, long ago, a chief of the clan called
Malcolm took a wife from among the fairy
people. She was both beautiful and kind, and
Malcolm loved her dearly. At first they were
very happy together, but after they had been
married for a year and a day, she grew sad
and longed to return to her own kind. For
fairy folk can never be happy for long in the
land of men. So Malcolm allowed her to go,
but she left behind her new-born baby son,

who was to be the next chief of the Macleods.

In Dunvegan castle, a great feast was held in honour of the new baby. It was an ancient tradition that the birth of the chief's son should be celebrated in this way, and the clansmen from far and near came to the castle. The baby himself was fast asleep in his cradle in a room high up in a turret of the castle. The young nurse who was caring for him could hear the sounds of pipe-music and dancing, laughter and merriment coming from the great hall below.

She couldn't resist going down to take a peep – she did not think any harm could come to the baby in a few minutes.

The baby, left alone in the turret room, began to cry. There was no one near enough to hear him, but his mother, away in fairyland, heard and came to him at once. But now she was a fairy once more, she couldn't pick the baby up and cuddle him, as a human mother could, and she stood looking sadly at her son in his cradle. Then, softly, she put over him an embroidered coverlet made of a piece of green fairy silk. And at once he went to sleep, and his mother went away.

Down in the great hall, Malcolm had noticed the nurse, and he told her to bring his son downstairs to show to the gathering. When the nurse climbed up to the turret room again, she saw the strange piece of silk on the cradle. It was embroidered all over with elfin

9

symbols, and she realised it must have come from fairyland. Yet the child seemed happy and unharmed, so she took him down to the hall, still wrapped in the green coverlet. As she carried the baby down the stone staircase, she could hear the voices of the fairy folk singing. And when she reached the hall, the whole company could hear the enchanted music.

The piping and the dancing stopped, and

everyone fell silent to listen to the song of the
fairy voices. They sang that the coverlet was a
fairy flag, a gift of the little people to the clan.
The fairy people would help the family as long
as the name Macleod existed. But the flag
was a special gift. Three times it could be
waved and the family of Macleod would be
saved from any danger which threatened them.
But it was to be used only with great thought
and care. If someone waved it for no good

reason, or just for a joke, a terrible curse
would come on the family instead, and three
things would happen. First, the son of the
chief would die. Second, a group of rocks at
Dunvegan would fall into the hands of the
Macleod's enemies. And third, a red fox would
give birth to her family in the turret room
where the baby had slept. That would be a sign
that the glory of the Macleods would vanish,
and they would lose their lands. There would
not even be enough men left in the chief's own
family to row a boat across Loch Dunvegan.

Then the singing stopped, and the company
stood staring at the baby and at the piece of
green silk that was so wonderful and so
terrible.

At last, Malcolm stepped forward and took
the flag. He gave orders that an iron casket
should be made for it, and that whenever the
Macleods went into battle, the casket should

go with them. But no one except a Macleod should be allowed to open the casket or to touch the flag.

In time, Malcolm died, and so did his son. Many hundreds of years passed, and the fairy flag remained safe in its casket. Then there came a time when the lands of the clan were attacked by a neighbouring enemy. A great battle raged, and as the day wore on the

Macleods were losing ground rapidly. It seemed as if they must be beaten. Then the Chief of Macleod remembered the flag and the promises about it, so he sent for the iron casket. He unlocked it and took out the little piece of green silk. Then he waved the flag aloft, in front of his men. Immediately, the enemy were driven back. This was the first time the fairy power was used.

Many years later, it was used again, this time for a very different reason. A plague of cattle sickness swept through the land, and the clansmen, having watched so many of their beasts die, came to the chief for help. So the casket was sent for and the flag unfurled – and the cattle recovered.

Time passed, and the flag in the casket was handed from father to son and the legend with it. But eventually some people began to scoff at the story.

Then, in 1799, a man called Buchanan who
had been left in charge of the castle while
Macleod himself was away, decided he would
like to test the power of the flag. For him it was
only an ancient piece of rotting silk, and the
legend only an old fairy story. The casket was
locked, but there was an English blacksmith
in the village, and he was sent for to break it
open. Then Buchanan waved the flag – for no
good reason at all.

15

What happened next *might* have happened
anyway, but it did seem as though the curse
of the fairy folk had been set in motion. In a
short while, the heir of Macleod was drowned
at sea. And the group of rocks at Dunvegan
were sold to a family who had once been great
enemies of the Macleods. Then, after some
time had passed, a young man was staying at
Dunvegan castle, and he was given the turret

16

room. He had a pet fox, and the fox had some cubs in the room. And, swiftly and surely, the fortunes of the Macleod family began to decline. Much of their land was sold, and gradually fewer and fewer Macleods were left. And one year, there were only three members left in the chief's own family – not enough to row a four-oared boat across the loch.

If you go to Dunvegan Castle today, you can see a square piece of ancient silk, now brown with age. And that is the fairy flag – or so everyone in the castle believes.

The Battle of the Birds

Once upon a time the birds of the air gathered together to have a great battle with the creatures of the earth. The son of the King of Tetherdown said he would go and see the battle, and bring back news to his father. For he wanted to know who would be king of the birds and beasts that year.

When the young man arrived it was nearly over, but a great black raven and a serpent were still fighting. It looked as if the serpent would win. When the King's son saw this, he decided to help the raven, and with one blow of his sword he cut off the serpent's head.

As soon as the raven got his breath back, and saw that the serpent was dead, he said:

"For your kindness to me this day, King's son,
I will show you a sight. Come up now and sit
on my wings."

And he took the King's son on his back and
flew up over seven bens, and over seven glens
and over seven mountain moors, until they
saw below them a fine house.

"That house belongs to my sister," said the raven, flying down to it. "Go there now, and she will make you welcome. Should she ask you if you were at the battle of the birds, say that you were. And should she ask if you have seen me, say that you did. And be sure to meet me here tomorrow morning."

The King's son did as he was told, and was treated very well that night. He was offered every kind of meat and every kind of drink. He had warm water to bathe in, and a soft bed to lie in. And the next day the raven took him again on his back, and again they flew over seven bens and seven glens and seven mountain moors. And again they reached a house where the King's son was made welcome. But the next morning, instead of the great black raven, the King's son saw a handsome lad with a bundle in his hand.

"I was your raven," said he, "but I was

under a spell, and meeting you has broken it. As a gift in return, take this bundle, and go back to your father's house. But be sure you do not put the bundle on the ground until you get to the place where you want to live."

The King's son thanked the lad and took the bundle, and then set off towards his father's house. He walked and he walked, and it seemed as though the bundle was growing heavier and heavier. He was passing through a thick forest when he felt he could carry it no

21

longer, and he put down the bundle to look inside. Immediately, a huge castle sprang up, surrounded by green orchards and gardens. It was a very fine castle, but the King's son didn't want his home in the middle of a thick wood. Yet he had no idea how to put the castle back into the bundle. As he stood wondering what to do, he saw a giant coming towards him.

"That's a bad place to build your house, King's son," said he. "What reward would you give me for putting it back in the bundle?"

"What reward would you want?" asked the King's son.

"I want your first son when he's seven years old," said the giant.

"Very well," replied the King's son. "If I have a son, I will do as you ask."

In a twinkling the giant put the castle back into the bundle and gave it to the King's son.

23

"Remember your promise," said he. "Should you forget, I shall still remember," and he went on his way.

When the King's son was near his father's house, he put the bundle down in a pleasant green hollow, and out of it sprang a castle as splendid as before. He opened the castle gate, and there saw a pretty lass coming to meet him. He asked her to marry him and they settled down to live happily in his castle. Soon he was King of Tetherdown, and father of a fine family.

When seven years had passed, the giant returned to remind him of his promise. The King's eldest son was nearly seven years old. He had no wish to give him to the giant, but a promise is a promise, and the giant stamped his foot so that the whole castle shook. So the giant took the eldest son to his house, and brought him up as if he were his own.

One day, when the giant was away from home, the boy heard singing coming from a room at the top of the giant's house. He climbed the stairway, and there he found the youngest of the giant's three daughters. She was very beautiful, and the boy fell in love with her at first sight.

When the giant came home, he sent for the boy. "Son of the King of Tetherdown," said he,

"I've looked after you well all these years that you've lived in my house. Now, you may choose either of my two elder daughters to marry. Which one will you have? The eldest?"

But the boy said he would have the youngest, the pretty one. His answer made the giant very angry.

"Before you can have her there are three things you must do," he said sternly. Then he took the lad to a cattle byre where a hundred cattle had been kept for seven years. "You must clean this byre by tonight," he said. "It must be so clean that a golden apple can roll from one end to the other. If it isn't cleaned by dark, you shall not marry my little daughter, instead you shall die."

The lad began to clean the byre, but he might as well have tried to sweep the sand from the seashore. By mid-day he was worn out, the sweat was pouring in his eyes, yet the byre

27

seemed as dirty as ever. Then the giant's youngest daughter came to him, telling him to rest and that she would help. Straight away he fell asleep. When he awoke in the evening, the byre was so clean that if a golden apple had been rolled from one end to the other, it would not have been marked.

When the giant saw it, he gave the lad his next task. This was to thatch the roof of the byre with birds' feathers – and no two feathers were to be the same colour.

The boy rose up with the sun next morning to go out onto the moors to search for birds' feathers. By mid-day he was worn out, the sweat was pouring in his eyes, yet he had found only two feathers and both of them were black. Then again the giant's youngest daughter came to him and said she would help, and again when he awoke in the evening all the work was done.

Then the giant named the third task. The
boy had to climb a fir-tree – the tallest in the
country, five hundred feet high – and bring
back the eggs from a magpie's nest on the
topmost branch. And again, by mid-day he

could climb no further, and the giant's youngest daughter came to his aid. She climbed to the very top of the tree, but when she was at the nest she heard the giant coming home. In her haste to get down again, she scratched her little finger until it bled.

But the tasks had been done, and that evening the giant arranged a great wedding feast. And what a feast it was! There were giants and lords and gentlemen, and such dancing and singing that the giant's house shook.

At midnight, the giant brought in his three daughters, all dressed alike and with their faces covered, and told the lad to choose his bride. Now this was hard, for all three girls looked exactly the same. But then the youngest daughter put out her hand, and at once the lad recognised her scratched little finger, and claimed her for his bride. The giant was angry,

but there was nothing he could do, and he
stamped off to his room.

"We must leave at once," said the giant's
daughter. "We must go before my father can
think of some new way to prevent it. Go and
saddle the grey horse, and I will play a trick
on him." And then she took an apple and cut
it into nine pieces. She put two pieces at the
head of the bed and two pieces at the foot, two
at the door of her room and two at the outside

door, and one in the garden. Then the prince and his bride mounted the grey horse and away they rode.

When the giant woke, he called out: "Are you asleep?"

"Not yet," said the apple at the head of the bed.

After a while, he called again: "Are you asleep?"

"Not yet," said the apple at the foot of the bed.

A little later, he called again: "Are you asleep?"

"Not yet," said the apple at the bedroom door.

Yet again, he called: "Are you asleep?"

"Not yet," said the apple at the outside door.

Then the giant shouted: "You are running away from me!"

"Not yet," said the apple in the garden.

At that the giant leapt from his bed and stormed out of the house. But the grey horse was gone, and his daughter and the prince with it, and he could do nothing.

At last, the King's son arrived at his father's castle with his bride. The giant's daughter said to the King's son: "Go to your father and tell him about me. I will wait for you outside the gate. But remember, let no one kiss you, for if this should happen you will forget me."

The King's son was given a great welcome
in his father's house, but he asked that no one
should kiss him. Before he had time to explain
why, an old greyhound which remembered
him jumped up and licked his face. And
immediately the King's son forgot the giant's
daughter.

The poor girl sat beside the well where the
King's son had left her, waiting for him. At
last, a good shoemaker and his wife took her

into their cottage to live with them. The giant's daughter worked about the house and helped the couple in all kinds of ways.

One day a young servant came from the castle to ask the shoemaker to make a pair of wedding shoes for the King's son. He was to be married that very day. When the shoes were ready, the giant's daughter begged to be allowed to take them up to the castle herself, so that she could get a peep at the King's son.

35

The servants took the girl into the wedding
room and filled a glass of wine for her. When
she put the glass to her lips a flame sprang
from it, and from out of the flame flew a
golden pigeon and a silver pigeon. They were
flying about the room when three grains of
barley fell on the floor. The silver pigeon
dived down on them and ate them up fast, but
the golden pigeon said: "If you could
remember when I cleaned the byre you
wouldn't eat without giving me a share."

Then three more grains of barley fell on the floor, and again the silver pigeon flew down and ate them. "If you could remember when I thatched the byre," said the golden pigeon, "you wouldn't eat without giving me a share."

Another three grains fell, and the silver pigeon ate them too. "If you could remember when I climbed the fir tree," said the golden pigeon, "and hurt my little finger that hurts still, you . . ."

At that, the King's son remembered everything. He ran to the giant's daughter and kissed her. As soon as the priest came, they were married, and all the court rejoiced at the wedding of the King's son and the giant's youngest daughter.

Diarmaid of the Shield

There was once a time when a band of warriors known as the Host of the Fianna lived among the people of the north. Many stories are told about them, some say they lived in Ireland, some say Scotland. The warriors of the Fianna were immensely tall and strong – almost giants – and their leader was Finn MacCoul. He wasn't the strongest of the heroes, but he was the wisest. He had a magic tooth of wisdom – he had only to touch it to know the answer to any question in the world.

Finn's nephew, whose name was Diarmaid, was one of the greatest heroes of the Fianna. He was often called Diarmaid of the Expert Shield because he was so clever at fighting with a sword and shield.

When Finn had been leader of the Host of the Fianna for many years, and they had fought many battles together and won many victories, he decided that he wanted a wife. Finn wanted a bride who was both beautiful and clever, and so fit to be the wife of the leader of the Fianna.

The Earl of Ullin had a beautiful daughter Grania, and Finn went to visit her at her father's castle. He wanted to test her wisdom. So he asked her some questions – questions something like riddles.

"What is more plenteous than the grass?" he asked.

Grania answered at once: "The dew, for there will be many drops of it on one blade of grass."

"What is blacker than the raven?" he asked.

"There is death," she answered.

39

"What is whiter than snow?" he asked again.

"There is the truth," she answered.

Then Finn asked his last question: "What is redder than blood?"

"The face of a good man when strangers come to his house and he has no food to offer them," answered Grania.

She had answered each of Finn's questions wisely and without any hesitation. He thought she was as clever as she was beautiful, and so

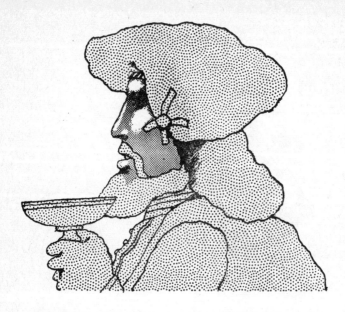

fit to be his wife. A splendid wedding feast was
arranged, which was to last for seven days
and seven nights. All the Fianna were there,
and among them was Diarmaid. Now Diarmaid
was the most handsome of the heroes. But he
always wore a cap, pulled well down on his
head, for high on his cheekbone he had a
magic love spot. He had been told that its
magic was so powerful that if any woman saw
it she would at once fall in love with him.

41

During the wedding feast, Grania's two white hounds started to fight over a bone that had been thrown on the ground, and Diarmaid knelt down to part the dogs. As he did so, the cap slipped from his head, and the love spot was uncovered. And at once Grania fell in love with him. Later, when Finn had fallen asleep, Grania came to Diarmaid and told him of her love. "I will go with you Diarmaid, to the far-off-end of the world," she said.

Diarmaid knew it was wrong to take Finn's bride away from him, and would not go. But then Grania put three spells of love on Diarmaid – one in his eyes to make him see what she wished him to see, one in his mouth to make him say what she wished him to say, and one in his heart to make him think what she wished him to think. And when Diarmaid looked at her again, his love for her was greater than his fear of disgrace.

While Finn slept, Diarmaid and Grania left the wedding feast and rode away together as far as they could go, for Diarmaid was ashamed. They hid in a big cave in the forest of Cloom. Finn was angry when he found they had gone, and sad too. He loved his nephew, but he could not forgive him for stealing his bride. He pressed his magic tooth, and straight away he knew where they were hiding. So, with his warriors, he set off to find them and kill Diarmaid.

Now all the warriors of the Fianna had sworn an oath that if they heard the sound of Finn's hunting horn they would go to him at once – wherever they were and whatever they were doing. So when Finn was near the great cave in the forest, he took his hunting horn and blew it.

As the sound echoed within the cave, Diarmaid remembered his oath, and said to Grania: "There is no help for it, beloved. I have sworn to answer that call, and I must go to Finn."

Grania was afraid that Diarmaid would be killed, and tried to stop him, but she could not stop him answering the call. When Finn saw Diarmaid, his anger died away a little. He could not bring himself to kill Diarmaid in front of the Fianna, as he had meant to do. So he decided to set him a task.

44

In the forest nearby lived an old woman who kept a herd of swine. The herd was guarded by a ferocious wild boar. Many of the heroes had gone to hunt this awful creature, but none had returned. So Finn sent Diarmaid to fight it. Diarmaid took his spear and his shield, for the boar was large and fierce, with great white tusks that could kill a man, and with sharp bristles a foot long on its

46

back. There was crashing and bellowing in
the forest when Diarmaid found the boar.
The heroes waited anxiously – they wondered
if Diarmaid would be killed. But Finn pressed
his magic tooth, and then he knew that
Diarmaid could only die by being cut on the
sole of his foot, and in no other way.

At last the fighting ceased, and Diarmaid came out of the forest dragging behind him the huge body of the dead boar. All the heroes cheered him, for he was a great fighter and a great favourite.

One of the warriors shouted to him: "Valiant Diarmaid of the Expert Shield, how big is the monster? Lay him on the ground and measure him. Walk along his back and count the paces!"

So Diarmaid, in his bare feet, paced out the
boar from tail to snout. "Sixteen feet of true
measure," he called out.

Now Finn knew that the boar's bristles
were poisonous, and if one should pierce
Diarmaid's foot then he would die. So he said
to Diarmaid: "Measure it again, walking
backwards, and I will give you a jewel for
every foot of its length." And Diarmaid began
the walk again, but before he had gone halfway,

one of the bristles pierced the sole of his foot and he fell to the ground. When Finn saw that he was dying he was sorry for what he had done, and cried out: "Diarmaid, is there anything which could make you well?"

"Some water from your own hands, Finn MacCoul, is all that can help me now," said Diarmaid.

Finn went to the edge of the loch to fetch some water. As he scooped up the water, he remembered his beautiful bride Grania and how Diarmaid had stolen her, and the healing water trickled through his fingers. He thought of Diarmaid and how brave he was, and then again he put his hands in the water. Yet as he remembered the wrong Diarmaid had done, once more he let the water trickle through his fingers.

A third time he tried to forget his anger and cupped his hands, but by the time he got back

with the water, Diarmaid was dead.

"I have killed my sister's only son," said Finn sadly. "One of the best of the heroes has died by my hand." And all the warriors who had fought beside Diarmaid and counted him as their friend, stood silent and sad. And Grania, when she heard what had happened, died from sorrow. The heroes dug a grave for Diarmaid and Grania beside the grey waters of the loch. They built a great mound to mark the spot, and laid the bodies in a long boat. Near Diarmaid they put his spear and his famous shield.

Many places in Scotland have been named as the burying place of Diarmaid and Grania. A few years ago, some workmen building a new road in a very lonely part of the highlands, discovered an ancient grave. The bones in it seemed to be those of a man ten or twelve feet tall. They left everything untouched and sent for some professors from Edinburgh to come and examine the remains. But on the next day there was no trace of the grave. And so no one knows where Diarmaid and Grania were buried, and long may it be so.

The Soldier's Tale

Once upon a time there was a soldier called John. He had been in the army for so long he was bored with it, so one day he decided to desert – to run away from the army. Now that was a very serious thing to do – so serious that in those days, if deserters were caught, they were shot.

John knew this very well, but it made no difference to him. His regiment was stationed in a little town among the hills in Scotland and, when no one was looking, John walked out of the camp. He went up a hill out of the town, and did not stop until he got to the top.

From there he looked down at the town and the army camp. He was so glad to have got away without being seen, he said out loud:

"May the Mischief himself carry me away on his back if ever I come anywhere near this town again."

And off he walked into the hills. He walked and walked until it was nearly night, and he began to wonder where he could stay for the night. Then he came to a gentleman's house.

"Can you give me a bed this night?" he asked.

"Are you a brave man?" said the gentleman.

"I'm an old soldier, and I've never yet been frightened," said John.

"You have the look of a man of courage. Do you see that castle beside the wood? You can stay there the night, for it belonged to my father. Since he died, no one has been brave enough to spend a night there, for it is said to be haunted. If you have the courage to try, I will see that you have a pipe and some tobacco, a glass of whisky, a Bible, a

54

comfortable chair, and a bed to sleep in."

"Agreed," said John. "I'm not the man to be afraid."

So after supper John went to the castle, lit a big fire to keep him cheerful, and sat in the chair with his pipe and his whisky.

After a while, there was a noise at the castle door and in came two women carrying a chest between them. They put down the chest near John and, without saying a word, went away again. John got up and kicked the side of the chest till he put his foot through it, and then pulled out of it a poor old grey man. He sat him in the chair by the fire and gave him his pipe of tobacco, but the old man let it fall to the floor and it broke.

"Poor man, you're cold," said John. So he made him comfortable a little nearer the fire, and there the old man stayed. When the cock crowed, he stood up and silently took himself off.

In the morning the gentleman came to see how John had spent the night. "Did you sleep well?" he asked.

"Very well," said John. "Your poor old father wasn't the kind of man to frighten me."

"I'll give you two hundred pounds if you're brave enough to remain another night," said the gentleman.

"Agreed," said John, "I'm not the man to be afraid."

So that night, after John had settled

56

himself comfortably in the chair by the fire,
there was a noise at the castle door and in
walked the same two women carrying the
chest. They set it down near John, and then
went silently away. Again John kicked in the
side of the chest and brought out the old grey
man. He put him in the chair by the fire and
gave him the glass of whisky, but the old man
let it fall.

"Poor man, you're cold," said John. And he

made him as comfortable as he could near the fire.

In the morning when the old man had left, the owner of the castle came to ask John what sort of night he had spent. As John seemed not a bit afraid, he offered him three hundred pounds if he would stay in the castle for a third night. "Agreed," said John, "I'm not the man to be afraid."

And that night everything happened as

before. But when it was near morning, and
near the time when the old man would be
leaving, John took from his haversack (that's
the pack that soldiers carry on their backs) a
leather strap, and strapped the old man to the
chair so he couldn't leave. Then the old grey
man spoke and begged John to let him go.

But John said, "I gave you a pipe of
tobacco, old man, but you dropped it on the
floor and broke it. I gave you a glass of whisky,

old man, but you dropped that and let it break. I've treated you well, but I'll not let you go till you've paid for the damage you've done."

Then the old man told John that in the cellars below the castle there was some buried treasure – silver, whisky, and tobacco. "Give some of this treasure to my son," said he, "and take some for yourself – but give plenty of what's left to the poor. I was hard and cruel to the poor when I was in this world, and I stole from them and cheated them – and now I cannot rest at night."

So John untied the old man and let him go. And when the castle owner came in the morning, John told him what the old man had said. When they went to the cellars below the castle, they found three rooms full of treasure – so John took his share and went on his way.

He went home to the town where he was

born, but after a time he was tired of it there
and would rather have been back with his
fellow soldiers in the army. So he put his
haversack on his back and set off to rejoin his
regiment. As he neared the town where the
regiment was, whom should he meet but the
Mischief himself.

"So you've come back, John," said he. "I'm
the Mischief, and you gave yourself to me
when last you were here."

"I've heard of you often," said John, "but I've never seen you before. How do I know you're the Mischief? Make yourself into a snake, then I'll believe you." And the Mischief did so.

"Now make yourself into a roaring lion," John ordered. And the Mischief did so.

"Well," said John, "if you're the Mischief and I'm to be your servant, make yourself so small you can jump into my haversack and

I'll carry you. But you mustn't come out, or the bargain is broken."

So the Mischief promised, and made himself small and jumped into the haversack.

John went down into the town to find some of his brother soldiers. And as soon as he was seen in the town, people started to recognise him and say: "There's John, the deserter." Before long he was caught and taken to the Colonel. He knew what his punishment would be, there was only one punishment for deserters. He would be put before a firing squad and shot.

All this time the Mischief, shut up in John's haversack, was wondering what was happening. He started to jump up and down, saying: "Let me out of here! Let me out, I'll soon settle these soldiers!"

"Hush, hush," said John. "Quietly, quietly."

"What's that in your haversack that you're

63

talking to?" asked the Colonel.

"Oh, it's only a white mouse," said John, about to open the haversack.

"Black or white I'm frightened of mice, so don't let it out here. Be off as quick as you can, I'll give you a letter of release and you may go free."

So John went free, still with the Mischief in the haversack on his back. He walked till he came to a smithy, where there was a huge furnace and twelve blacksmiths were working. There was a great noise from the banging of the twelve hammers and the roar of the flames in the furnace.

"Where are we now, John?" called the Mischief. "What's all that terrible noise?"

"A little patience and you'll see," replied John.

"Let me out, let me out!" called the Mischief. "If you'll only let me out, I'll

64

promise never to trouble you again in this world."

"Nor in the next?" asked John.

"I agree," called the Mischief.

But John didn't trust his promises, so he threw the haversack into the furnace, and Mischief and all went up in a great green flame into the sky. And after that, John went back to the army and joined his brother soldiers again.

The Black Bull of Norroway

Once upon a time, there lived in Norroway a woman who had three daughters. Norroway is the country we call Norway now. But long, long, ago, Norway and Scotland may have been joined together, and certainly several of the stories told in the two countries are very much the same. This story has been known in Scotland – and in parts of England too – for hundreds of years.

The woman and her daughters were happy enough, but they were poor, and seemed to have no hope of getting richer. So one day the eldest daughter said to her mother: "I'm going away to seek my fortune. Bake me an oatcake

and roast me some meat. I shall ask the
wise-woman where I should go."

The wise-woman told her to look out of the
back door of the house and see what she could
see.

The first day she saw nothing.

The second day she saw nothing.

But on the third day she saw a coach and
six horses coming along the road. So she ran to
the wise-woman and told her. "That's for

you," said the wise-woman. So the girl stepped into the coach and off she went.

The second daughter said to her mother: "I'm going away to seek my fortune. Bake me an oatcake and roast me some meat. I shall ask the wise-woman where I should go."

And the wise-woman said to her: "Look out of the back door of the house and see what you can see."

And after three days, she saw a coach and six horses coming along the road.

"That's for you," said the wise-woman, and in she stepped and off she went.

Then the youngest daughter said to her mother: "Now it's my turn to go away and seek my fortune, Mother dear. Bake me an oatcake and roast me some meat. I shall ask the wise-woman where I should go."

And the wise-woman gave her the same advice as she had given her sisters.

68

But looking out of the back door of the
house on the third day, the girl could see
nothing but a great black bull which came
roaring along the road. "Well," said the wise-
woman, "that's for you." The girl was terrified,
but she was lifted up onto the back of the
black bull and away they went. Long they
travelled and on they travelled till the girl
grew faint with hunger.

"Look in my right ear," said the bull, "and you will find food, and look in my left ear and you will find drink," and so she did. After that the lass felt better.

On they travelled and hard they rode till they came in sight of a castle.

"My brother lives here," said the bull, "and here we will stay this night."

The servants took the girl into the castle and put the bull into a field for the night. They

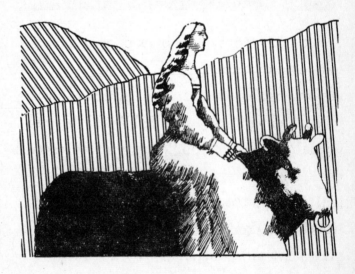

treated her very well, and in the morning they gave her an apple. They warned her to take care of it, and told her not to break it open until she was in trouble and needed help. Then the apple would help her. She thanked them and took the apple, and off she went again on the back of the bull.

That night they came to another castle, and the bull stopped and said: "My second brother lives here, and here we will stay this night."

Again they were treated well, and in the morning the girl was given a pear. The servants told her to keep it until she was in need of help. She thanked them and took the pear, and off she went again on the back of the bull.

On the third night the bull stopped at a third castle, where his third brother lived. And while the bull was put in a field, the girl was well-treated in the castle. And in the morning she was given a plum, and told not to open it till she needed help. Then she got on the back of her friend the bull, put her arms round his neck, and off they rode. Long they rode and on they rode, till they came to a dark and ugly glen. There the bull stopped and the girl got down.

"You must stay here and wait for me," said the bull. "I must go and fight a demon. Sit on that stone, and move neither hand nor foot till I return, or I'll never be able to find you again. If everything about you turns blue, I'll have won the fight, if it turns red, I'll have lost."

So she sat on the stone hoping that the bull would win his fight and come back soon, to find her.

And before long everything about her turned blue. She was so excited that she crossed one foot over the other, quite

forgetting the warning the bull had given her.
Long she sat on the stone in the dark glen
alone – until she was wearied with waiting.
At last, she thought if the bull could not find
her, she could try to find him, and she set off
across the world to look for him. She wandered
on and she wandered long until she came to a
great hill made all of glass. She tried to climb
it, but she could not even begin.

Nearby she found a blacksmith working, and

she thought that if she had a pair of iron shoes she could climb the glass hill. So she asked him to make her some. He said he would, if she stayed in his smithy and worked for him for seven years. Seven years' work was a hard price to pay, but at the end of that time he gave her the shoes. He told her if she wanted to find what she was seeking she must first go to the washer-wife's cottage. So she climbed the hill of glass, and came to the cottage.

There she was told about a gallant young knight who had come to the cottage after being wounded in a battle with a demon seven years ago. The knight had asked that his shirt, all stained with blood, should be washed by the washer-wife. The old wife washed and washed until she was tired, and then she let her daughter wash, but the shirt would not come clean. At last they let the stranger lass try, and at once the shirt was white.

The old wife told the young knight that it was her daughter who had washed the shirt so white and the knight said he would marry the daughter as soon as his wounds were healed.

The stranger lass was distracted when she heard this, for she knew that the knight was really her friend, the bull, for whom she had been seeking for so many years. Suddenly, she remembered the apple she had been given, so she broke it open and found it was full of precious jewels.

"All these are yours," she said to the washer-wife's daughter, "if you will let me nurse the wounded knight for one day."

The daughter agreed, but she gave the knight a sleeping draught so that he slept all through the day. The girl sat by his bed and wept and sang this song:

"Seven long years I served for you,
The glassy hill I climbed for you,
The blood-stained shirt I wrung for you,
Will you not waken and turn to me?"

But the young man slept and slept. The next day she remembered the pear that had been given her, and found it was filled with jewels even richer than before. So she bargained again, and the same thing happened. While she sang, the young man slept. And she nearly lost hope. But as the knight woke from his deep sleep, he thought he could remember hearing someone singing in his room. He determined that the next time he was given a drink by the washer-wife's daughter he wouldn't take it.

Meanwhile the lass broke open the plum, and found this held the richest jewels of all three. So she bribed the washer-wife's daughter again, and she sat by the young man's bed and sang as before:

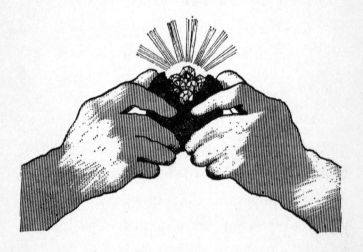

"Seven long years I served for you,
The glassy hill I climbed for you,
The blood-stained shirt I wrung for you,
Will you not waken and turn to me?"

The young knight understood her song and
turned to her. And they recognised each other.
She told him all that had happened to her
since he left her sitting on the stone in the dark
glen. And he told her all that had happened
to him since he had fought the demon and
was turned into a man again, and how he had
looked and looked for her and could never
find her.

So she nursed him till he was well again,
and they married and lived happily ever after.

Other books in the Jackanory series:

Arabel's Raven
The Barrow Lane Gang
Brer Rabbit Stories
The Elm Street Lot
Dragons
Jack Stories
Icelandic Stories
Islands
The Lion and other Animal Stories
Littlenose
Littlenose Moves House
Littlenose the Hero
The Quest for Olwen
Robin Hood
The Saturday Man
Stories from Ireland
Stories from Poland
Stories from Russia
Stories from Wales
Voyage of the Griffin
The Wilkses

Records

Also obtainable are the BBC Roundabout records of favourite Jackanory stories—Roundabout Nos 5 and 7. Recommended retail price 99p from your local record shop.